**FRIENDS
OF ACPL**

# The Little Drummer Boy

# The Little Drummer Boy

Words and Music by Katherine Davis, Henry Onorati, and Harry Simeone

Illustrated by

## KRISTINA RODANAS

Clarion Books ✦ New York

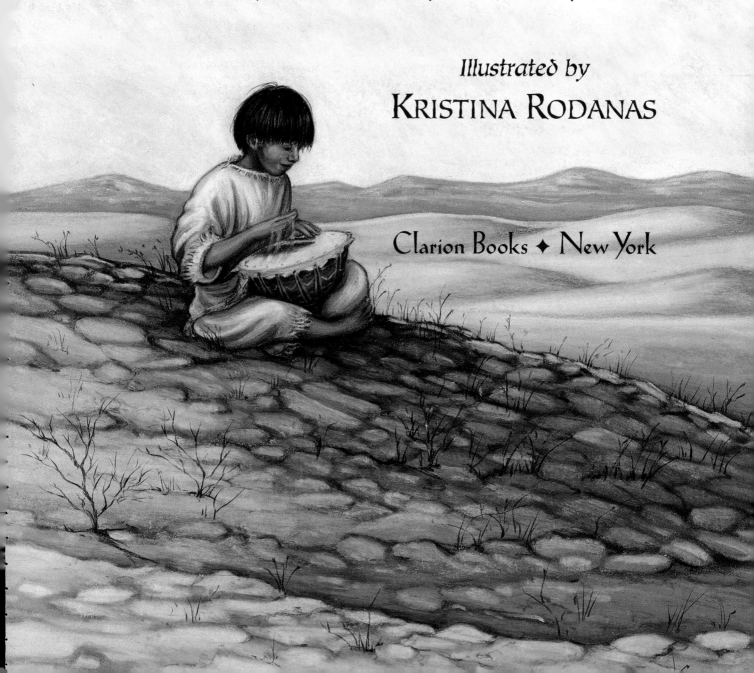

Clarion Books • a Houghton Mifflin Company imprint • 215 Park Avenue South, New York, NY 10003 • The Little Drummer Boy • Words and Music by Katherine Davis, Henry Onorati, and Harry Simeone • © 1958 (Renewed 1986) by EMI Mills Music, Inc. and International Korwin Corp. • Worldwide Print Rights on behalf of EMI Mills Music, Inc. • Administered by Warner Bros. Publications U.S. Inc. • All Rights Reserved • Used by Permission • Illustrations copyright © 2001 by Kristina Rodanas • The illustrations were executed in colored pencil and watercolor. • The text was set in 23-point Eva Antiqua. • All rights reserved. • For information about permission to reproduce selections from this book, write to Permissions, Houghton Mifflin Company, 215 Park Avenue South, New York, NY 10003. • www.houghtonmifflinbooks.com • Printed in Singapore• Library of Congress Cataloging-in-Publication Data • Rodanas, Kristina. The little drummer boy / lyrics and music by Katherine Davis, Henry Onorati, and Harry Simeone ; illustrated by Kristina Rodanas. p. cm. Summary: An illustrated version of the Christmas carol about the procession to Bethlehem and a poor boy's offer to play his drum for the Christ Child. • ISBN 0-395-97015-6 [1. Carols, English—Texts. 2. Christmas music—Texts. 3. Carols. 4. Christmas music.] I. Onorati, Henry. Simeone, Harry. Davis, Katherine. II. Title. PZ8.3.R614 Li 2001   782.42/1723 E 21   00-047455

TWP   10  9  8  7  6  5  4  3  2  1

For Greg, with love.

Special thanks to Asa and Briana Larsen, and to
Eleanore von Thaden, who was born on Christmas Day.

—K. R.

Come, they told me, pa-rum pum pum pum,

Our newborn King to see, pa-rum pum pum pum,

Our finest gifts to bring, pa-rum pum pum pum,

To lay before the King, pa-rum pum pum pum,
rum pum pum pum, rum pum pum pum,

So to honor Him, pa-rum pum pum pum,

10

When we come.

Baby Jesus, pa-rum pum pum pum,

I am a poor boy too, pa-rum pum pum pum,

I have no gift to bring, pa-rum pum pum pum,

14

That's fit to give a king, pa-rum pum pum pum,
rum pum pum pum, rum pum pum pum,

Shall I play for you, pa-rum pum pum pum,

On my drum?

Mary nodded, pa-rum pum pum pum,

The Ox and Lamb kept time, pa-rum pum pum pum,

I played my drum for Him, pa-rum pum pum pum,

I played my best for Him, pa-rum pum pum pum,
rum pum pum pum, rum pum pum pum,

24

Then He smiled at me, pa-rum pum pum pum,

Me and my drum.